For Sydney and Olivia

ANN ESTELLE STORIES

Queen of Easter

BY MARY ENGELBREIT

HarperCollinsPublishers

very year Ann Estelle's neighborhood had an Easter Parade. And every year Ann Estelle got a new hat to wear in the parade.

This year Ann Estelle wanted a hat with flowers. She wanted pink and purple ribbons that hung all the way down her back. She wanted a hat that would make her

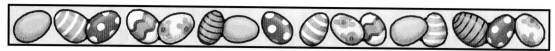

But her mother bought her a plain straw hat with a blue ribbon. One blue ribbon. One short blue ribbon. *And nothing else.*

"I sn't it pretty?" said Ann Estelle's mother. "So classic." Ann Estelle didn't say a word.

She took her new hat out on the porch. She put it on and tried to like it. But she just couldn't.

"Ann Estelle!" her father called. "Dinner!"

Ann Estelle set her hat down on the porch railing.

"I cannot be the Queen of Easter *with a hat like this,*" she said.

And she went inside.

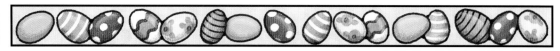

 few days later, when Ann Estelle came downstairs, her mother and father were very excited.

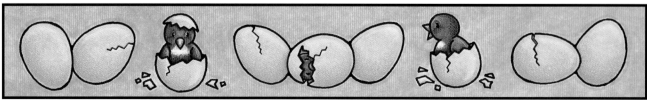

"Come here!" her mother whispered.

Ann Estelle was surprised.

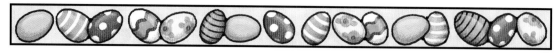

here, still on the porch railing, was her new Easter hat. Inside the hat was a bundle of sticks and grass and bits of string. And on top of the bundle was *a robin*.

"It's a nest," whispered Ann Estelle's mother. "She built a nest in your Easter hat!"

Ann Estelle certainly couldn't wear her new Easter hat now!

"I'm sorry, honey," said her mother. "You'll have to wear last year's hat. Maybe we can put a new ribbon on it."

That gave Ann Estelle **an idea.**

 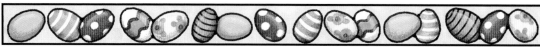

The next day Ann Estelle took her old Easter hat and went to work. She glued and she stapled. She snipped and she sewed.

Not just one new ribbon but lots of them—long pink and purple ribbons. Lilies and daisies. She put some plastic grass on top too.

But that was just a start.

very day when she came home from school, Ann Estelle checked on the nest. Soon there were *three tiny eggs*. They were the most beautiful blue she had ever seen.

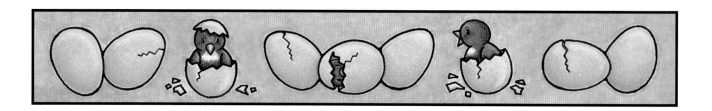

o, when Ann Estelle went to work on her old hat, she stuck three tiny light blue candy eggs on it. It was getting closer and closer to a hat that could belong to *the Queen of Easter.*

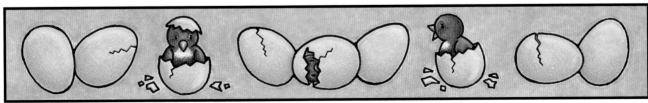

A week before the Easter Parade, the eggs in the nest

hatched.

Every day Ann Estelle watched the baby robins get bigger and stronger. Their voices grew louder. It was as though they were excited about spring too.

On the morning of the Easter Parade, Ann Estelle put on her pretty new dress. Then she put on her old, newly decorated hat.

 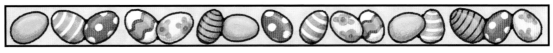

It was *so heavy* she had to hold her head up very carefully. But, as fabulous as her old hat was now, Ann Estelle knew there was an even better one.

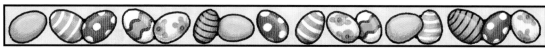

Outside, everyone was getting ready for the neighborhood Easter Parade. Everybody was wearing bright new clothes and big smiles.

EASTER PARADE STARTS HERE

I nside, Ann Estelle was **busy working.**

When the parade got to Ann Estelle's house, she called everyone over.

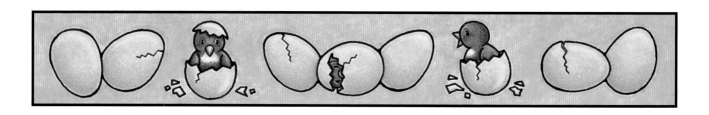

"Look," she said, pointing to the singing birds. Her sign said it all—

"The Very Best Easter Hat Ever!"

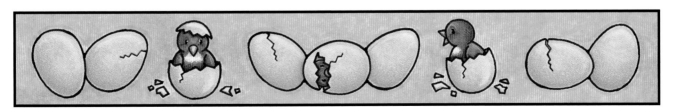

Queen of Easter
Copyright © 2006 by Mary Engelbreit Ink
Manufactured in China.
All rights reserved.
No part of this book may be used or reproduced
in any manner whatsoever without written permission
except in the case of brief quotations embodied in critical articles and reviews.
For information address
HarperCollins Children's Books, a division of HarperCollins Publishers,
1350 Avenue of the Americas, New York, NY 10019.
www.harperchildrens.com

Library of Congress Cataloging-in-Publication Data is available.
ISBN 0-06-008184-8 — ISBN 0-06-008185-6 (lib. bdg.)
Typography by Stephanie Bart-Horvath
1 2 3 4 5 6 7 8 9 10
❖
First Edition